For Daisy and Kate

ORCHARD BOOKS
338 Euston Road, London NW1 3BH
Orchard Books Australia
Hachette Children's Books
Level 17/207 Kent Street, Sydney, NSW 2000
10 digit ISBN: 1 84121 589 9
13 digit: 978184125891
First published in Great Britain in 1999
This edition published in 2001
Copyright © John Butler 1999
The right of John Butler to be identified as the author and illustrator of this work has been
asserted by him in accordance with the Copyright, Designs and Patents Act, 1988.
A CIP catalogue record for this book is available from the British Library.
2 3 4 5 6 7 8 9 10
Printed in Singapore

While you were Sleeping

John Butler

ORCHARD BOOKS

While you were sleeping one deep, dark night, animals all around the world were stirring.

Some were near, some were far away, and they were waking, while you were sleeping on that deep, dark night.

While you were sleeping,
one tiger went hunting in the jungle.

While you were sleeping,
two mice made a warm,
cosy nest in the hay.

While you were sleeping,
three bears played
chase in the snow.

While you were sleeping,
four baby owls sat wide-eyed
in an old oak tree.

While you were sleeping,
five dolphins leapt out
of the deep, blue sea.

While you were sleeping,
six deer jumped over a silvery stream.

While you were sleeping,
seven geese flew silently
past the moon.

While you were sleeping,
eight rabbits played in
a misty meadow.

While you were sleeping, nine elephants marched through the long grass.

While you were sleeping,
ten penguins jumped
out of the icy sea...

...where they met one hundred penguin friends, and all while you were sleeping, warm and safe.